D1509623

The Frannie Shoemaker Campground Series

Bats and Bones

The Blue Coyote

Peete and Repeat

The Lady of the Lake

To Cache a Killer

The Space Invader

Also by Karen Musser Nortman

The Time Travel Trailer

Trailer on the Fly

Happy Camper Tips and Recipes

a campy christmas

A Frannie Shoemaker
Campground Adventure

by Karen Musser Nortman

Cover Artwork by Aurora Lightbourne
Cover Design by Libby Shannon

Dedicated to the Spirit of Christmas

Wherever there is a human in need, there is an opportunity for kindness and to make a difference.

Kevin Heath

Kindness is like snow--it beautifies everything it covers.

Croft M. Pentz, *The Complete Book of Zingers*

Sign up for Karen's email list at
www.karenmussernortman.com and receive
a free ereader download of *The Blue Coyote*.

TABLE OF CONTENTS

CHAPTER ONE
Blue Christmas/White Christmas

FRANNIE SHOEMAKER LOOKED around her empty, drab house. It seemed warm and cozy the rest of the year, but in December with no tree or flamboyant decorations, it felt more like a cell. This was the first year of her forty-four year marriage to Larry that she had not put up a tree. It was going to be okay; she was now sure of that. Back in October, their son Sam had told them that Beth and he were taking the children to Disney World for Christmas. Sarabeth and Joe were the Shoemakers' only grandchildren, so their absence would put a hole in Frannie's Christmas. But she'd had time to come to terms with it. After all, Sam and Beth had to make some of their own memories and traditions.

Then a week ago, their daughter Sally called, her voice filled with excitement. She was a social worker in St. Louis and had a new man in her life, Brett. She had planned to bring him home for a week at Christmas and introduce him. That was the carrot that had kept Frannie from being too down about Sam and Beth's absence. But Sally's call had changed all of that.

"Oh, Mom! Last night, Brett gave me my Christmas present early! And you'll never guess what!"

Frannie's heart filled with joy for her daughter. Sally wanted to be married and have a family but had never found the right guy.

"A ring?" Frannie squeaked.

Sally scoffed. "No, silly, we aren't ready for that. He's taking me skiing in Switzerland!"

Frannie readjusted. "That's wonderful, honey. When?"

"Over Christmas. We leave the 23rd and won't be home until the second week of January. I'm sorry we won't be coming for the holidays but we'll come up for a weekend the end of January or early February."

And like that, the lights went out of Frannie's Christmas.

It hurt that, in Sally's eyes, a weekend later was as good as a week during the holidays. Since it was just going to be adults this year, Frannie had made dinner reservations at a new restaurant and bought theater tickets. She had decorated the house, with special touches in Sally's old bedroom. She was just about to put up the tree when Sally's call came.

Larry was much more matter-of-fact. "We'll still get to meet him, just a little later. We can ask someone else to dinner and the theater."

Frannie put her fists on her hips. "Who, Larry? Everyone else we know will be busy with family."

"Then we'll go by ourselves."

"Merry Christmas." She turned on her heel, and stalked into the living room to haul the boxes of tree decorations back to the attic.

The exercise was therapeutic. By the time she had climbed the steps six times, lugging heavy boxes and refusing Larry's help, she had cooled down and tried to be realistic, as well as happy for Sally. When Frannie was young, her father had been killed in the Korean War. The rest of her childhood, Christmas was just her and her mother. After her marriage, she reveled in the hectic holidays with her own children and Larry's large and boisterous family. But this year, Larry's only nearby sibling and Frannie's closest friend, Jane Ann Ferraro, and her husband, Mickey, were headed to their brother Bob's place in Texas. Everyone else had made other plans.

She still didn't want to put up the tree but tried to look at it as a special Christmas for her and Larry. She also reminded herself of the meaning behind the hoopla and threw herself into helping at the homeless shelter and the senior citizen meal site. She thought more positively and began to anticipate the holiday, until at weekly coffee, a friend mentioned special plans for her six grandchildren coming for Christmas, and another described her upcoming visit to her children and grandchildren.

Her spirits sank. She felt such a loss — she knew it was foolish. She told Larry maybe they should go somewhere else to celebrate — do something entirely new. They discussed the possibilities.

The week before Christmas, they invited Jane Ann and Mickey to join them for supper before the Ferrarros' departure for Texas. Frannie had only spoken with Jane Ann briefly since Sally's call.

"So, what are your plans?" Jane Ann said, over a plate of turkey thigh stew.

"Just the two of us," Frannie said, trying to sound upbeat. "We thought we might go somewhere but haven't decided." She glanced at Larry, who was deep in an argument over football with Mickey.

"So why don't you go with us?"

"What?"

"Sure." Jane Ann put down her fork. "Bob would love to have you and I know Justine wants to see her Aunt Frannie and Uncle Larry. Then we're going to do a little camping in West Texas and New Mexico, maybe even Arizona."

Larry had honed in on their conversation and looked at Frannie. "Why don't we? We talked about going somewhere."

"But, our trailer is winterized and in storage. I emptied everything out of it."

"Well, stay with us then," Mickey said.

Jane Ann and Frannie looked at him and then at each other and burst out laughing.

"Thanks for the offer, Mick, but the thought of you and Larry in the same space for even a few days does not bring up visions of peace on earth and good will to men. Or their wives," Frannie said.

"You're leaving Thursday?" Larry said to Mickey.

"That's the plan. We'll take two days to go down and get there Christmas Eve. We found a private campground in southern Missouri that's open year round and has heated showers and restrooms, so we won't need water hookups. I'll call them tomorrow and see if they have room for one more."

Frannie's mind whirled. She was getting excited. A trip and still spending Christmas with family—just what she wanted.

"So what are you doing about food?" she asked Jane Ann.

"We thought we'd just eat out on the way down and then stock up down there. I put in staples and a few frozen dishes we can heat up if we need to."

Larry said, "What do you think, Fran? Be impulsive and keep it simple?"

She smiled at him, her face glowing. "Why not?"

THE NEXT TWO days were a whirlwind. Larry brought the trailer back from the storage barn and Frannie packed clothes and restocked the cupboards. She always kept the condiments in a plastic box in their old garage refrigerator so it was simple to move them back to the camper. She threw in the canned goods she had on hand—some beans, vegetables, and broth. Pints of homemade tomato sauce went in the camper's freezer.

She usually baked treats and muffins before each camping trip, but time didn't permit that. Fortunately, she had cranberry bread in the freezer, peanut clusters in the refrigerator, and paper-thin sugar cookies dusted with red and green sugar already made. Bread, milk, and lunchmeat completed the necessities. They could survive anything.

Then Frannie turned to the house. She didn't want to come home in a few weeks to sad-looking decorations, so she picked out a few special ones to take along and packed the rest up. Meanwhile Larry and Mickey pored over forecasts and watched the Weather Channel with the same rapt attention they usually reserved for ESPN.

She made up the RV's bed with flannel sheets and a thick red plaid comforter. Even in the South, nights could be cold at this time of year. She hung a lighted copper star in the kitchen window and a little artificial greenery and red berries on the wall lamp.

A tree—even a small one—wasn't practical in a moving camper, so she decided a string of white rope lights fastened along the top of the slide-out extension would have to suffice. A few Christmas CDs and the weather radio went in the entertainment cabinet. And her two favorite Christmas mugs went in the mug basket.

To choose a travel wardrobe, she followed the 'rule of five' described by a friend over coffee: five of each clothing item. Two pairs of jeans, two of sweat pants, and one of corduroys. Two hooded sweatshirts, two bulky sweaters, and one ugly

Christmas sweater. And so on. Her ratty old parka, as well as Larry's, was stored under the bed, along with mittens, stocking caps, boots, and extra blankets.

They stopped the mail, donated the theater tickets to the young couple next door (who were thrilled), and made arrangements for their old yellow Lab, Cuba, to stay with their sometimes-camping companions, Ben and Nancy Terell. Between phone calls to Jane Ann, she filled water jugs to take along. She and Larry had never taken their camper out in the winter, so she figured it was better to be safe than sorry.

They turned off the water to the house, turned down the furnace, and locked up the house. With a last look around the quiet, chilly house, she knew she was ready for some adventure.

CHAPTER TWO
Dashing Through the Snow

IT WAS ABOUT a six-hour drive to the campground that the Ferraros had lined up in southern Missouri, not allowing for gas, bathroom stops, and lunch. An Arctic clipper was forecast to move across Iowa in the middle of the day, so they were anxious to get going ahead of it. Mickey and Jane Ann led in their Class C motorhome, the 'Red Rocket.' Frannie kept an eye on the heavy gray sky to the west and constantly checked the radar on her iPad.

Jane Ann called Frannie's cell. "Mickey says he wants to get south of Des Moines before we stop. Will that work for you guys?"

Frannie relayed the question to Larry, who peered at his gas gauge. "It'll be close, but I think we can make it. Tell her we'll call if we need to stop sooner."

By the time they reached Des Moines, fine sleet was starting, but they soon drove out of it and made it to a truck stop not far from the Iowa-Missouri border. After filling their gas tanks and their coffee mugs and emptying their bladders, they put their heads together over Frannie's iPad to watch the track of the storm.

"It looks like it's swinging a little farther south," Mickey said.

Anytime Mickey spoke in a serious tone, it worried Frannie.

Larry pulled up the forecast for central Missouri. "I think we'll be okay. They're still not predicting anything there."

They got back on the road, and in spite of Larry's reassurance, Frannie fretted over the radar. An hour later, they stopped at a fast food joint and took their lunch to go. Larry took the lead, and they were barely back on the road when rain started. Larry checked the outside temperature.

"Barely above freezing," he said, his voice thick with concern. "Hope it stays there."

The rain came down harder and the temperature hovered at 34° F. They still had a good two to three hours to their planned stop for the night. The sound of the precipitation hitting the truck changed from a patter to pings and the temperature began to drop. The wipers struggled to keep the windshield clear.

"Crap," Larry said. "It's starting to freeze." He slowed the truck slightly and gripped the wheel tighter as a little sideways slide of the trailer pulled at the truck.

"Call Mickey," he instructed Frannie. "We need to pull over—I just saw a sign for a rest stop up ahead. What's the radar showing?"

She activated the screen while she waited for Jane Ann to pick up. "There's a blue blob just west of us and looks like it's moving fast."

Jane Ann answered, and Frannie told her about the rest stop just as they reached the exit. It was an inactive rest stop and the building had been removed. All that was left was the lay by.

Mickey ran up to their truck, a stocking cap pulled down over his ears and his hands shoved in his pockets. He opened the crew door and climbed in the back seat.

"Whoo!" he said, catching his breath. "This isn't good."

Frannie held up the iPad so he and Larry could both see the blue blob.

"Whaddya think?" Mickey asked. "Wait it out here or try to find a campground?"

"It doesn't look like it's going to get any better soon. Frannie, pull up that campground app and see if there's anything close by here. We just passed a sign for a town called Rock City or Rockport or something." Larry pulled out the atlas from under his seat and examined the Missouri page. He put his finger on a spot.

"Here! A state park called Bender Woods. See if you can find out anything about that."

"Probably not open this time of year," Mickey grumbled.

Frannie scrolled through a list and chose the park.

"It is!" Frannie said. "It says year round camping. How far do you think it is?"

"Well, this rest stop is still marked on the map and it looks like the exit for the park is only about two miles. What do you think, Mick?"

He looked over Frannie's shoulder at the blob that was engulfing Missouri and Iowa.

"Think we can make it that far?"

"We can drive on the shoulder if we have to," Larry said.

"Probably not a good idea. But, you're right; it won't get any better if we wait. You lead." He exited the pickup and returned to his motorhome.

They edged onto the interstate. The traffic had slowed considerably. It was the longest two miles in Frannie's memory. An SUV and small sedan were in the ditch and a semi had jack-knifed in the median. Visibility was deteriorating. The throb of the wipers almost sounded like a warning, increasing the tension as they put all of their concentration on the road ahead.

Frannie realized she was gripping the armrest and tried to relax while watching for the exit sign.

Finally, it appeared out of the gloom, and she pointed. "Coming up!"

Larry pulled off slowly, Mickey behind him. At the top of the ramp, a sign indicated the park was to the right. Another mile down the less traveled, icy road and another turn took them onto gravel. The park entrance sign was the most beautiful sight Frannie could imagine. They pulled up along the registration shack and Larry and Mickey ran to the door and ducked inside. In a few minutes, they were back. Larry climbed in the driver's seat, brushed drops of water and ice from his head, and handed Frannie a slightly damp copy of a campground map.

"Well?" she said.

"Just like the Ritz," he said and pointed to two circled numbers on the map. "No one else is here — no surprise — so the ranger says to take these two sites right across from the bath house. Water and heat are on in the bath house and the electricity is on to the sites." He put the truck in gear and pulled forward. "She's about to lock up and leave. She lives in town and has kids so she will lock the gate and we have the whole place to ourselves. She gave me her cell number if we have an emergency." He pointed to a number on the bottom of the map.

"Really?"

"Really what?"

"We'll be kind of stranded out here?"

"We'll be fine. Better than on the road. We have phones and the internet. Okay?"

"I guess." Frannie gazed out at the icy rain.

"I figure we'll just leave the truck hooked up since it doesn't look like we'll be going anywhere tonight. Do we have anything to throw together for supper?"

"Sure," Frannie said. She definitely didn't want to go any farther in this mess, so they might as well make the best of it. She was looking for adventure, right?

SHE GOT OUT and directed Larry's backup into the site. It was a little more crooked than he would have liked, but they decided that on a day like this it really didn't matter.

Mickey pulled his coach in forward so that their doors faced. Shrouded with hoods and gloves, they scurried around completing the absolutely necessary chores, looking like the Jawa from Star Wars, had anyone been around to observe.

With the jacks down in the corners, Frannie hit the button to roll out the slide--the extension of their living and dining areas. She moved the lamp and TV from the bed to their rightful places and turned on the lamp to provide a warm glow on such a dreary day.

Larry came in, gently shaking drops off his slicker and hung it in the shower. He rubbed his crew cut and peered back outside.

"We stopped none too soon. It's changing to snow and on top of that ice, it's going to be a real mess. I told Mickey and Jane Ann to come over when they got set up."

"Good," Frannie said and put a soft Christmas CD on the player. She looked around and smiled.

"Cozy," she said.

Larry put an arm around her. "How many days' worth of food do we have, woman?"

Pounding on the door interrupted the romantic moment, and Mickey burst in, followed by Jane Ann.

"Break it up," Mickey said. "We're not standing on ceremony when the snow is coming down. Don't you have your TV hooked up yet, Shoemaker?"

"Yeah, right, the reception should be great," Larry said. "I'm ready for a beer. How about you?"

Mickey produced a jar of salsa from his coat pocket and Frannie opened a bag of chips. They settled around the little living room, relishing the protection from the growing storm.

"We should have some hot cider," Mickey said.

"Well, I was going to come down early and plug my crockpot in the shower house, but I forgot," Frannie said.

"Sarcasm doesn't become you," Mickey replied.

"Enough," Jane Ann said. "The first thing we need to do is call Bob. There's no way we are going to get there tomorrow, right? Even if they get the roads opened in the morning?"

"Probably not," Larry said.

"Ohhh, bummer. Tomorrow's Christmas Eve," Frannie said.

"He'll understand. He wouldn't want to lose his favorite siblings."

Jane Ann laughed. "I'm going to tell Elaine you said that."

"If you don't, I will," Larry said. "Seriously, there's nothing we can do, and if they're watching the weather, they're probably wondering why they *haven't* heard from us."

"I know," Frannie said, as she turned a taco chip around and around in her fingers. "I just feel bad about disappointing them."

"Maybe they'll be relieved," Mickey said. "Especially Lois." They all had mixed feelings about their sister-in-law but tolerated her for Bob's sake.

"Be that as it may," Larry slapped a hand on the table, "we must report in. If we get a signal."

"I have three bars," Jane Ann said and called up Bob's number. With that out of the way, they concentrated on what would be the highlight of their evening—supper.

CHAPTER THREE
Do You Hear What I Hear?

"WE HAVE SOME FROZEN meatballs," Frannie said.

"We could do spaghetti," Mickey said.

"Did you bring spaghetti?"

"No," said Jane Ann.

"Us either. How about soup? I have tomato sauce in the freezer and some veggies."

"Perfect," Mickey said. "If I had some buttermilk, I could bake some casserole bread."

Frannie snapped her fingers. "I have half a quart that I didn't want to leave at home or throw out. Is that enough?"

"You bet. Hand it over."

Frannie got it out and looked at her watch. "Two o'clock now. I can put the soup in the crockpot."

Jane Ann looked out the window. "Man. Look at the size of those flakes!"

"Looks like a Christmas card," Frannie said. "This is turning into a real adventure."

"Let's hope it doesn't turn into a tragedy," Larry said.

"Larry!" Jane Ann and Frannie both said.

"We have plenty of propane, right?" Frannie asked.

"Yeah."

"We have power."

"That could end any time in this kind of storm."

"Well, we have access to the shower house," Frannie persisted.

"If we can get there," Larry said, nodding toward the storm. "We should be fine but we need a plan. Whenever we use any water from our jugs, we need to get them refilled at the shower house as soon as possible. We also better get our battery lanterns on the chargers while we do have power, and the phones. We did bring the weather radio?"

Frannie nodded. "In the cabinet under the TV."

"Okay. How about this? You and Mickey work on supper and Jane Ann and I will check on supplies."

"Yessir!" Mickey saluted, receiving a slight frown for his efforts.

Frannie got out the crockpot. "Our boots and parkas are under the bed, Larry."

"I know," he said and grinned. "I checked."

Frannie turned to Mickey and Jane Ann. "You guys bring winter gear?"

"Of course," Jane Ann said. "I *am* my brother's sister, after all. I'm prepared for everything up to a meteorite hit."

Larry ignored her. "You know, it's certainly possible that something might go wrong with either of our campers and we would have to all hole up at the other one. Maybe we should both keep our emergency supplies near the door in case we have to transfer them."

Mickey rolled his eyes. "What if we get such a pile by the door that we can't get out in an emergency?"

"You won't need to worry, because I will murder you before then."

"Please don't say murder," Frannie said and shuddered, thinking of previous camping trips that had turned up dead bodies.

"Besides, not very appropriate for a retired cop to make threats of an illegal nature," Mickey said.

"Go make your bread," Larry said.

Mickey picked up the carton of buttermilk and pulled the hood of his windbreaker up. When he opened the door, a slice of cold air rushed in bearing ice pellets and snow. "Yikes!" He hurried out into the snow.

Jane Ann watched him go. "It is accumulating fast. Good thing Mickey isn't any shorter." But her face showed a little concern.

"We'll be okay," Frannie said with more confidence than she felt. "Does anyone know how far the nearest town is?"

"About seven miles," Larry said. Of course he knew. He was already getting out the lanterns. Soon every available outlet was sprouting at least one charger with a lantern, cell phone, or tablet attached.

Meanwhile Frannie busied herself dumping meatballs, tomato sauce, frozen veggies and garbanzo beans in the crockpot. She added garlic, Italian seasoning, and some onion. After adding water to the mix, she plugged in the pot to the only open outlet. She washed her hands and set the half-empty jug on the counter by the door to be refilled.

21

"Now. What can I do? I need to go to the restroom so I'll refill that jug. Do we need to fill any other containers?"

"How many do we have filled?" Larry asked.

"Four with that one," Frannie said.

Larry turned to his sister. "How many do you have?"

"Five, I think."

"We should be okay. We won't be stranded here more than a day or two. I hope."

"Okay." Frannie pulled on her boots and shrugged into her parka. Every time she looked out, the snow seemed to be thicker. Jane Ann got ready to go back to her own camper to ready her emergency supplies. Frannie pushed open the door and clambered down the narrow metal steps, then held the door for Jane Ann. Larry helped them get it shut, and Frannie gave Jane Ann a little wave as she struggled through the deepening snow to the shower house across the road.

The snow was about six inches deep so far and it covered a crust of ice, which made staying upright a challenge. A strong northwest wind whipped the flakes around, creating very poor visibility. When Frannie pushed the door open to the women's side, a miniature drift quickly formed on the floor at the doorway.

She turned on the water in the sink and opened the plastic milk jug. The shallowness of the sink precluded bringing the mouth to the faucet and filling it. She looked around. The showers were the type with a narrow pointed nozzle. That should work. She held the mouth of the jug up against the nozzle with her left hand and reached in to turn the handle with her right.

But as she turned the handle, she moved the jug just enough that the water hit the side instead of the mouth and shot out at her in a wide, forceful spray. She yelped and dropped the jug, backing up from the gush.

Her hair and jacket were soaked, her glasses covered with spray. She started to swear but caught a glimpse of herself in the mirror and burst out laughing. Paper towels got the worst of it, but her jacket and hair were still damp. They would need to devise a better way to refill the water jugs.

For now, she picked up the mostly empty jug and carefully held it back up to the nozzle and barely turned the faucet on. It took several minutes to fill. Her arm started to ache, but she managed to finish the chore. She pulled up her hood over her damp hair and headed back out into the storm. The poor visibility made her think of the stories where pioneers ran a rope from the house to the barn. Might be a good idea.

"What happened to you?" Larry said after she set the jug on the counter and started to take off her coat.

She launched into the tale, and he struggled to keep the smirk off his face. She stopped and then said, "Oh, no!"

"What?"

"After all that, I forgot to go to the bathroom." She put her coat back on and retraced her barely visible steps. Larry wisely didn't say anything.

By the time she returned, her face felt like it was coated with ice and she relished the warm camper with its fragrant aroma of soup. After finding her slippers and drying her hair, she fixed herself a mug of instant cocoa. Larry explained his collection of emergency equipment in a plastic bin by the door. He had also plugged in the little space heater to supplement the efforts of the camper furnace.

She settled on the couch with a fleece blanket, her cocoa, and a book. Larry raised the antenna and fiddled with the TV, finally giving up in exasperation. He turned the Christmas music back on and kicked back in his recliner with his own book.

"This isn't bad," Frannie said. "It certainly will be a Christmas we'll always remember."

Larry looked outside. "Let's hope it's fond memories."

But she wouldn't let his gloom-and-doom outlook ruin her contentment.

A short while later, they heard some activity outside the trailer. Larry went to the side window and looked out. He went to the door and opened it.

"Mickey, what are you doing?" A gust of cold wind prompted Frannie to wrap her fleece closer.

"Lighting the way!" she heard Mickey yell. She got up and went to peek around Larry. Mickey had run a string of rope lights along the ground from one camper to the other.

"I hate to say it, but not a bad idea," Larry said. "Sorry I can't stand here to visit."

"I understand," Mickey yelled. "We'll be back over soon."

Larry closed the door and they returned to their nests. The early dusk was closing in when Jane Ann and Mickey stomped in. More coats and mittens were draped in the shower and Frannie helped them with beverages. Mickey had placed his warm loaf of bread on the counter and the wonderful aroma mingled with that of the soup.

Frannie and Jane Ann started a game of dominos at the dinette while Larry and Mickey tried in vain to get anything on the TV and argued about every antenna adjustment.

Jane Ann arranged her dominos and raised her eyebrows at Frannie. "Have you noticed how their feuds have become comforting background sound, just like the music?"

Frannie laughed. "I hardly notice it—"

She was interrupted by a loud THUNK against the window right beside them. They both jumped. "What was that?" Even Larry and Mickey shut up.

Jane Ann peered out the window, down at the ground. "There's something down there but it's almost too dark to see. It might be a bird."

"Well, if it is, he wasn't very smart to try and get in the camper that way," Mickey said.

Jane Ann got up. "He's still moving. We can't leave him there."

"Jane Ann, he's wild. You can't help him," Larry said.

"How do you know it's a he?" Mickey asked.

"Because he didn't ask directions and ran into the trailer," Frannie said. She got up and got their coats out of the shower. They ignored their husbands' attempts to talk them out of it and they tromped out into the snow.

Mickey's lights were rapidly becoming covered with snow and looked like they were under gauze. Jane Ann reached down and jerked them back on top of the snow. They trudged around the trailer to the back. The wind bit at their faces. Frannie held a small flashlight in her mitten and they soon located the downed sparrow. It was on its back so Jane Ann tried to gently set it upright. It fell over on its side.

"Doesn't look like he can fly," Frannie said. "What are you supposed to do with them?"

"You're supposed to take them to a wildlife center," came Mickey's voice behind them.

Jane Ann stood. "Well, that's not really an option today."

"That's why I brought this out," Mickey said. He held out a small box lined with a paper towel. "Put him in here and we'll take him in to warm him up."

Fannie stood up and took the box from him. "Mick, you old softie."

"Someone had to help you girls out. I was a Boy Scout, you know."

Jane Ann carefully lifted the bird into the box. "Only for a month, until you were kicked out for selling Girl Scout cookies at a markup."

"Mick! You didn't!"

"No, I didn't because no one would buy 'em. Let's get that little guy inside." He turned and led the way back to the camper door.

Once back inside, Mickey poked holes in the box lid and covered the shaking creature. "We need to put this somewhere dark and warm. Do you have a heating pad?"

"Just my little rice bag," Frannie said. "If that will work, I'll heat it up."

"Should be fine."

They put the box back in the bedroom with the heated rice bag under it.

"Seems like we should try to give him a little water," Frannie said, when they came back out.

"According to an article I read, not a good idea. He may have a concussion. But the article doesn't say his caretakers shouldn't eat and drink." He looked longingly at the crockpot of soup.

"It is after 5:00," Frannie said. "I think that's close enough."

CHAPTER FOUR
The Friendly Beasts

Frannie and Jane Ann picked up the dominos and set the table with red plastic plates and bowls with red and green bandanas for napkins. Frannie added a little wrought-iron lantern tied with a piece of fat red yarn.

"Looks pretty festive, if I do say so myself," Frannie said.

Jane Ann snapped a photo. "Recorded for posterity."

Once they all squeezed around the dinette, Frannie said, "We certainly can't say we aren't cozy."

Mickey elbowed his wife. "For sure."

They exclaimed over the soup and warm bread and returned for seconds until both were gone. As Frannie heated water on the stove for dishes, she thought it would have been smarter to use paper plates and bowls, but after all, it was almost Christmas. Larry washed and Jane Ann dried, while Mickey fiddled with the weather radio. Frannie checked on their houseguest back in the bedroom.

"He seems comfortable enough," she reported.

Mickey finally managed to tune in to the emergency station. The robotic voice was giving dire snowfall and wind speed predictions by county.

"What county are we in?" Mickey asked.

"There's an atlas in that footstool," Larry said, his hands still in the sudsy water.

After locating the name, Mickey listened carefully until the repeated spiel covered their area. His eyes wide, he sat back.

"Blizzard conditions," he said. "Winds of forty miles an hour tonight."

"Oh, my," Frannie breathed. "That will make it hard to keep this place warm."

Larry wiggled his eyebrows. "Guess we'll just have to snuggle. And get out the extra blankets." He got his coat. "I'll go refill the water jugs before it gets any worse."

"Yeah, good luck with that," Frannie said. She and Jane Ann played another game of dominos. When Larry returned, the blast of cold air that accompanied him in made them scramble for blankets.

"Man!" He stomped his feet. "It *is* awful out there." He and Mickey joined the game and their good-natured arguments and complaints helped to drown out the howling wind. Frannie put out a plate of sugar cookies. But a whine and a scratching sound on the door permeated their consciousness.

Jane Ann accidentally knocked her dominos over. "What is that?"

"Sounds like an animal." Mickey got up and grabbed the flashlight. Larry followed him to the door and turned on the outside light. Mickey cracked the door and poked his head out.

"I don't see anything. There's tracks though." He pulled the door closed and they returned to the table. No sooner had they seated themselves than the scratching started again.

"Could it be a coyote or something?" Jane Ann said.

"Not likely. They're pretty skittish and wouldn't be scratching at the door."

Mickey got up and opened the door again. This time a black apparition hurtled in almost knocking him over. It whined and spun in a circle looking for the way out again.

"A dog!" Jane Ann said.

Larry held out his hand. "Here, boy," he said in a quiet voice.

"How do you know it's a boy?" Frannie asked.

"Because he came in to ask directions."

The dog ceased its circling and crawled over to Larry. It was medium-sized of indeterminate breed, its long black fur matted and wet. It had white feet and white markings on its face.

"Look at him shake," Jane Ann said.

Frannie got up to get an old towel. "Well, we can't put him back out in this weather."

"What do we have that he could eat?" Larry said.

"There's some lunch meat. That's about it unless you want to thaw out a couple of meatballs."

"Lunch meat will do." Larry took the towel from Frannie and coaxed the dog closer. He draped the towel over the dog's back and gently rubbed the fur while the animal gazed at him with soulful eyes.

"Looks like he doesn't have a collar or tags," Jane Ann said.

"I think he's in love with you," Mickey said.

"Then *he* must be a *she*," Larry answered.

Frannie got a couple of slices of lunch meat out and gave them to Larry. The dog snatched them up and then sniffed and licked Larry's hand looking for more.

"Poor guy — or girl. We're getting quite a menagerie," Jane Ann said.

"Oh, Larry! I didn't think about that. We can't have them both in here tonight," Frannie said.

Mickey kneeled on the floor by the dog and cautiously reached out his hand. "We'll take the bird over to our place. If he makes it through the night and looks like he can fly, I'll put the box out under the eaves of the shower house tomorrow. We can still keep an eye on him."

"Unless we get out of here tomorrow," Frannie said.

"Then we can turn him over to the ranger."

They agreed that was the best plan. Larry found a bowl and poured some water from one of the jugs into it, which the dog greedily lapped up. Mickey determined that the dog was indeed a female.

"I think we should call her Dasher because of her entrance into the camper," Jane Ann said.

Larry fiddled with the iPad. "Hey, I've got some reception. The weather site isn't good news though.

The blizzard warning extends through tomorrow afternoon." Just then the lights flickered, accompanied by a crash of thunder.

Mickey groaned. "Thunder snow. That's even worse news."

The dog raised her head, looked around, and whined. They waited for the power to fail completely but nothing else happened. Larry put the recharged battery lantern on the counter, just in case.

Frannie checked her phone. "A message from Sam—two hours ago." She opened it. "Said they tried to call and they're having a great time. I forgot to tell him we wouldn't be home." She laboriously typed in a reply and sent it off. "Now it says 'No service.'"

"I think we should head for our coach while we still can," Jane Ann said. "I know I'm ready for an early night."

"I think we all are." Frannie gave Jane Ann a hug. "Stay warm."

While Mickey and Jane Ann got their coats and boots on, they were all surprised by the ring of Larry's phone. As he picked it up, he said, "We must have reception again." His conversation was very brief with mostly one-syllable answers except for reassuring the caller they were fine.

"Who was that?" Frannie asked when he hung up.

"Kelly Hart—the ranger. She said the roads are closed and just wanted to make sure we were okay. Said she'd call again in the morning if she can't get here."

Mickey wrapped the box with the bird in an old towel, generating considerable interest from the dog. Readied, they opened the door, keeping a tight grip on it so the wind wouldn't take it. Frannie saw that Mickey's lights were almost buried again and Jane Ann pulled them back above the snow as they trudged toward their coach, which was barely visible even though it was only about thirty feet away.

After they left, Larry said "Want to be my bathroom buddy for one last trip tonight?"

"That's kind of personal but probably a good idea. I can't see the shower house even thought it's right across the road." They too donned their parkas and boots.

Dasher stood up and looked at them expectantly. "Hold your horses," Larry told her. "I'll take you out when we get back."

She seemed to understand, circled a couple of times, and dropped back on the floor with a sigh.

The snow was still blowing almost horizontally, and Frannie clung to Larry's arm as they plodded across the road. They were halfway across before the building loomed into sight. The light at the front of the building was out, so when they reached the front, they separated and Frannie stayed close to the cement block wall until she got to the door of the women's side. She relished the running hot water. After she finished, she exited and followed the wall again to the center of the building where Larry waited for her.

Once they got close to the trailer, Larry pointed at the roof. "Somehow, tomorrow, we're going to have to get some of that snow off of there, and especially the slide," he yelled over the wind.

When they got inside, she said, "We don't have any kind of ladder, do we?"

"No. Maybe Mickey does. Or when the ranger calls, I can find out if there's one we can get to. There's that door in the middle of the shower house that's probably a utility or supply closet but we'd have to break in. C'mon pooch—let's get this done."

"We don't have a collar or a leash."

"If she runs away in this weather, she's not very smart and there's nothing we can do. But I don't think you need to worry."

Sure enough, when he returned in a few minutes, Dasher launched herself into the camper ahead of him and burrowed into the old towel they had laid on the carpet for her. Larry laid his gloves on a register to dry and shed his coat again.

"You would think the wind would keep the snow off the roof," Frannie said.

"Normally it would but we had that freezing rain first and that's probably holding some of it up there. You, know, there was an odd thing in the men's restroom. A ratty old blanket was on the bench. I don't remember seeing it there earlier."

"Really?" Frannie considered. "Are you sure?"

"Pretty sure. Either Mickey or I would have noticed it."

"No one else checked in after we did, did they?"

"I don't know how they could have. The ranger was going to lock up. Just kind of strange."

Frannie looked out the window, which was useless because she couldn't see a thing. "Spooky."

She found her warmest pajamas and a pair of heavy socks for good measure. She hadn't thought to take her toothbrush to the bathhouse, so she used a little of the jug water for that chore. Larry turned down the furnace to save propane. They switched off the lights in the living room and soon were burrowed under the blankets and comforter.

"I think I don't even want to have my hands outside the covers to read." Frannie leaned over and turned out her light. She pulled the covers up to her chin and lay there for a while listening to the wind and wondering about an explanation for the old blanket. The thought made her tense, and she nearly jumped out of her skin when something landed with a thud in the middle of the bed.

"What—?" She sat up and switched her bedside lamp back on. Larry had done the same. There in the middle of the bed was Dasher, looking very pleased with herself.

Frannie laughed and tried to calm her heart. "Obviously she's not well trained. Get down!"

Larry said, "Maybe we should leave her. We may need each other's warmth before the night is over."

Frannie snuggled back down. "Okay, but she better not ever tell Cuba." They had never allowed any of their dogs on the bed.

The wind continued to howl and batter the side of the camper, but the presence of the stray dog was strangely reassuring, and she soon drifted off to sleep.

CHAPTER FIVE
Bring a Torch, Jeanette, Isabella

IT WAS STILL dark when Frannie woke. Really dark. It took her a moment to realize that the soft snores beside her were coming from the dog, not Larry. And then another few minutes to realize the reason it was so dark was that the nightlight in the living room was not on. The bulb might have burned out, or more likely the power had gone off — not a good thought.

She got up, shivered, and grabbed a hooded sweatshirt. In the living room, she checked the space heater — not running. No lights on the microwave either. So the power was definitely off. She curled up in the recliner with a fleece throw and mentally checked off what that meant.

None of the outlets would work. The 12V ceiling lights would still operate, the fridge would switch to propane, and the stove was also propane. The water heater could run on gas but since they had no water in the tank, that didn't matter. The microwave was out but the furnace was propane. Fortunately they wouldn't need the AC.

She turned on one of the ceiling lights and looked at the wall clock—5:30. That meant coffee. But she couldn't use the percolator or make instant in the micro. Mickey and Jane Ann had a generator and would no doubt fire it up but they wouldn't be awake for a while.

She was getting out a saucepan to heat water for instant when she remembered her 'flower pot.' She kept an old stovetop percolator under the sink and used it for flower arrangements for the table. And every time that she took the basket and stem out of it, she wondered why she didn't just throw them away. Now she knew why. After filling the pot and the basket, she folded back the stove cover and lit one of the burners. While waiting for the pot to perk, she checked the phone and the iPad. No reception.

There was a thunk sound from the bedroom, and Dasher poked her nose around the curtain.

"C'mon, girl." Frannie sat on the couch and patted the seat. Dasher jumped up and snuggled next to her.

"You don't know how lucky you are," Frannie whispered. "*None* of our dogs ever have been allowed on the furniture or the bed."

When the coffee finished, she turned off the burner and got out one of the Christmas mugs and poured a cup. It was a little strong and slightly gritty. But since a half hour before, she had thought she might have to do without for a couple of hours, it was the best coffee she had ever tasted. She wrapped her hands around the bright red mug and looked at the dog.

"So where did you come from? Is someone looking for you?" The dog cocked its head at her as if it was considering how to answer the question.

"And, you know, you would have been smarter to have found a nice warm farmhouse with a well-stocked fridge. We might end up as bad off as you were last night."

No answer, so she picked up her book. After a few minutes, she closed the book on her thumb to save her place and leaned her head back. Christmas Eve morning. It seemed less and less likely that they would be getting out of this park today. Hopefully, they would know more when the ranger called.

And what about the shower house? Did the plumbing depend on an electric pump? It might be a good idea to bring in a couple of buckets of snow to supplement their water supply. They could subsist several days on lunchmeat sandwiches but it would be nice to do something special for Christmas Eve. She was sure they could concoct *something,* but dozed off before she could decide what that was.

SHE WOKE WITH a start when the dog jumped off the couch and barked.

"Hey, pooch—don't bark at me. I'm the hand that feeds you, remember?" Larry stretched and got out a coffee mug. He glanced at the counter where the electric percolator usually sat.

"The power's off. I made some coffee in that little pot but it probably needs to be reheated." She got up and removed the basket and the stem from the pot. Larry lit the burner and turned it low.

"How long has it been off, do you know?"

"No idea. It was off when I got up. Do you think that will affect the water in the shower house?"

"We'll find out soon enough." He reached for his coat and gloves. "I'll take the dog out and then head over there." He leaned over to see out the window. "Hard to tell if the snow has let up, because it's still blowing."

"I'd better join you." She turned off the burner. "We'll reheat it when we get back."

Encased in coats, boots, gloves, and hats, they headed out. Frannie got to the bottom of the steps and stared at the ground.

"Huh. Footsteps going by our camper." She looked up at Larry.

"Ours from last night."

"I would think they would be covered over by now. And they only go one direction." The frolicking dog quickly obliterated all of the prints, squatted gingerly in the snow, and was ready to go back in.

As they plodded across the road, the wind whipped Frannie's pajamas around her legs and made her eyes water. She just about ran into Jane Ann coming out of the restroom.

"Good morning! Although the news isn't good. The water's off."

"We were afraid of that. Is it warm?"

"Not bad — but I don't think the heat is working so it'll probably get colder as the day goes on. Each of the toilets will flush once, so I think we need to fill five-gallon buckets with snow for future use."

"Good idea. We've got a couple. We'll chat later." Frannie's teeth were chattering and she pushed open the door.

"Yeah — too cold here!" Jane Ann headed back to her camper.

BACK IN THE trailer, Frannie told Larry about Jane Ann's suggestion.

"What? Oh, sure. I'm going to have some cereal and then I'll get the buckets out of the truck."

"I'll help. Think I'll put about three layers of clothes on first."

When she came back out of the bedroom, Larry was staring out the window, his cereal only half-eaten.

"Everything okay?"

He gave her a half smile. "As all right as everything can be when we're snowbound out in the middle of nowhere with no power."

She squeezed his arm. "I heard Mickey's generator start up so I bet he will have some real coffee and that will help. And we aren't really all *that* far from civilization."

"We'll see." He checked his phone. "Nothing yet from the ranger. If she doesn't call by the time we're ready to go out, I'll call her."

Frannie fixed herself some cereal. If Larry was worried, she was worried.

He got his coat on. "I think there's part of a bag of dog food in the truck from last time Cuba came along. I'll get it."

When he returned, Dasher obviously recognized the scent and pranced around with anticipation. Frannie refilled her water dish too, just as Larry's phone rang.

"Yes?" he said. "I see. The power is off here too. Okay for now. But we're concerned about the snow on the roofs of our campers. Is there a ladder anywhere we can get to? Okay, thanks."

He put the phone back in his pocket.

"Doesn't sound like good news," Frannie said.

"There's a couple of big trees down on the park road. No one can get through and they brought down the power lines as well. The governor has declared an emergency so they'll probably be bringing in some guardsmen to help."

"Great. What about a ladder?"

"The only ones she knows of are in a maintenance building on the other side of the park." He rubbed his crew cut. "I think we need to unhitch the truck, and maybe we can pull it alongside the trailer and clear some of the snow that way."

"Oh, bummer. Nothing's ever easy, is it? Too bad we don't have a unit with one of those ladders on the back."

"Well, if wishes were horses…"

"I know, I know." She picked up her coffee mug. "Let's go see if Mickey has coffee made yet and we can make a plan for the day."

CHAPTER SIX
Up on the Housetop

MICKEY ORDERED THEM in with "close the door behind you!"

Frannie inhaled the heavenly aroma of good coffee and held out her mug. "Can I have some more, please, Sir?" she asked in a meek voice, a la *Oliver!*

"Certainly, my sweet! You know Oliver would have done better if he had been Olivia."

"How's the bird doing?"

"He doesn't look great, but he is still alive. I don't want to put the box outside until this wind dies down."

Larry plopped down on the couch and reported on his call from Ranger Hart. The mood sobered. But Mickey was never down for long.

"So! A plan! We need a plan!"

"I think the first order of business is to get some buckets of water into the shower house to melt for flushing the toilets," Jane Ann said.

Mickey checked off an imaginary list.

"And then the camper roofs," Larry said. "I'm really worried about our slide. Frannie and I will unhitch the truck and I can use it to climb up on and at least get the slide cleared. You have a ladder on the back of the coach, don't you?"

"We do, but I'm going to need a boost from your truck. The bottom is pretty far off the ground."

"We have brooms," Jane Ann said. "Do we have any shovels?"

"One little one with our fire tools set," Larry said. "It will have to do."

"Wait, I put in one of those short ones for digging cars out," Mickey said. "I mean the handle's short, but the shovel part is decent sized."

"Okay, we also need to melt snow for drinking water, and we need to turn our furnaces down to conserve propane and battery power. Anything else?" Larry said.

"Anybody been able to get any Internet reception this morning?" Frannie said.

Mickey raised his hand. "Me! Me! The blizzard warning is still out for most of the day but the snow is supposed to be tapering off. Cold though."

"Okay, any other problems we need to work on?" Larry was about to adjourn the meeting.

"Food!" Mickey said.

"I assume we have enough to get by."

"Get by, yes, but tonight is Christmas Eve. If we're still stuck here, we should do something special. Now, Frannie what's in your larder?"

"Wellll—I have more of those frozen meatballs, and some chicken breasts that I was going to grill for my lunch salads."

"Lunch, shmunch!" Mickey slapped the table. "Have a peanut butter sandwich. Okay, chicken, meatballs—what else? Any vegetables?"

"Um, some frozen broccoli, peas, and I think Brussels sprouts. What are you contributing?"

"We have some shrimp and chorizo I was taking to Bob's for an appetizer and breakfast burritos. But if we ever get there, they have grocery stores in Texas."

"So what are you making?" Frannie persisted.

"It's a surprise. It's Christmas, you know, my sweet." He reached over and pinched her cheek.

Larry got up. "Okay — time for chit-chat later."

"Why don't we take care of filling the buckets while you and Frannie unhitch the truck?" Jane Ann said. "Then we can all work on the camper roofs."

"Good idea." Frannie pulled her coat back on.

THE SNOW DID seem to be abating, but the wind worked effectively with what it had. Frannie let the dog out and grabbed her camper keys from above the door. Before they could unhitch, they had to put the wheel locks in, and those were stored in one of the outside compartments. Once that was done, they removed the sway bars, and Larry raised the jacks a bit to allow him to raise the front lift and take the trailer off the hitch. Once level again, he lowered the jacks.

He stomped his feet and rubbed his gloved hands together. "Let's go in and warm up a little and then I'll move the truck. We need to move that picnic table in the next site and it may take all of us if it's frozen to the ground."

Dasher was as eager as they were to return to the relative warmth of the trailer. Mickey and Jane Ann came over, having finished their assignment. Frannie sipped her lukewarm coffee and wished for the power to come on long enough to reheat it. Right.

As they tromped back outside, Larry hung back and talked to Mickey in low tones.

"Something's really bothering Larry, and he won't say what it is," she told Jane Ann.

"He's just worried about what could happen, even if it's not likely. He's always been a glass-half-empty guy."

"Maybe."

They gathered around the picnic table on the backside of the Shoemaker trailer. The first attempt to lift it produced no results.

"It's frozen to the ground," Mickey said. "Maybe if we try jerking it to loosen it first..." and he demonstrated, while the others joined in. At first, their efforts seemed fruitless and Frannie's arms began to ache. But then a sharp crack split the air and it broke loose. They dragged it over far enough that Larry could back the truck near the slide.

"Just don't hit the electric post, in case the power comes back on," Mickey said.

"Thanks for the warning, Mick. Never thought of that."

Once the truck was moved with the help of the four-wheel drive, Larry got out a board that he carried for leveling, placed it across the bed of the truck, and climbed up on it. Frannie handed him

Mickey's little shovel and he started to work on the slide.

Since the slide cantilevered out from the side of the trailer and had no support under it, the extra weight on the roof was worrisome. The snow was wet and packed. Larry strained and grunted to scoop even a little off. Frannie pulled another board out of the storage compartment and Jane Ann helped her put it across the truck bed near the other end of the slide. She grabbed one of the brooms and climbed up on the tailgate and then onto the board. Jane Ann hung on to the other end of the board and warned her about stepping too close to the end.

They were just beginning to make headway went Frannie felt her perch jolt and heard Larry let out an "Oof!"

She turned just enough to see globs of snow cascading off Larry's coat. In the background Mickey stood looking up, both gloved hands covering his mouth.

"Damn it, Ferraro, can't you ever quit?" Larry yelled. He turned around and glared at Mickey. "How did you plan to take care of me if I fell off and broke my leg?"

It came out almost whiney, which was not at all like Larry, but Frannie could see that he was furious.

He knew something he wasn't telling them, and it was keeping him on edge.

Mickey came around between the truck and the trailer. "Man, I'm sorry. Wasn't thinking, I guess."

"When do you ever? Aren't you a little old for snowballs?" He attacked the snow on the roof more aggressively and a large chunk broke loose, flew off the slide, and hit Mickey in the face.

Frannie had been standing with her mouth open. She and Jane Ann were used to Larry and Mickey's constant banter, but this was the first time she had ever seen Larry really angry with his brother-in-law. Now, watching Mickey paw the wet snow off his face, she started to giggle and Jane Ann burst out laughing.

Larry steamed for a moment longer and then couldn't keep a straight face.

"That was on purpose!" Mickey blustered.

"I don't think so," Jane Ann managed to get out, "but if it was, you deserved it."

"Oh, Mickey," Frannie gasped. "If we had that on video, we'd all be rich."

Mickey grinned. "See, I can't count on you guys for anything."

"You'd better go get dried off," Jane Ann told him. "Actually, we could probably all use a warm up."

"I'm almost done with the slide," Larry said, working the shovel.

Mickey moved away from the trailer.

INSIDE, THEY STOMPED their feet and blew on their hands.

Larry said to Mickey. "It shouldn't take long to get enough off the rest of our roof to remove any danger of collapse, and then we'll work on yours. I think the snow has stopped — it's not filling up the tracks as fast."

That reminded Frannie. "Weird thing this morning — when we were headed to the bathrooms, there were tracks coming up to the camper."

"Yours from last night?" Jane Ann asked.

"No, there was only one set. And it was still snowing hard when we came back last night so they would have filled up." Frannie leaned back against the couch and rubbed Dasher's head. As she did so, she caught a look between Larry and Mickey.

"What?" She sat up straight. "What is it, Larry, that you don't want to talk about?"

Larry sighed and leaned his elbows on his knees. "I didn't want to scare you, but I guess it's better that you know so you can be alert. Remember I mentioned last night that there was an old blanket on the bench in the men's side?"

Frannie nodded.

"Well, it was gone this morning. I asked Mickey, and he didn't move it. Someone else is here."

They sat silently for a few moments, each processing the implications of that information.

"Do you think someone was lost? But surely they would knock on the door or have seen us outside," Jane Ann said.

"Maybe a kid? A runaway?" Frannie hugged the dog to her. "Someone who doesn't want to be found?"

"The next time one of us gets Internet reception, check for local news to see if anyone's missing," Mickey said.

"Or escaped," Frannie said.

Larry grimaced. "I doubt if it's something like that."

Frannie tilted her head. "Then why were you worried?"

"I'm not worried just about that—just the weather and the power and everything. That said, let's go get the snow off the other camper and be done with that."

IT TOOK THEM the rest of the morning to finish the job. When Frannie was standing on the bed of the truck, she occasionally scanned the woods behind the campsites. Was someone out there? There really was no other explanation for the blanket disappearing. But she saw nothing. Mickey and Larry were on the roof of Ferraros' coach, and it seemed prudent to keep an eye on them in case they decided to send an avalanche her way.

Mickey decided he could take their little feathered friend in his box to a sheltered side of the shower house and prop it in the eaves. That done, they feasted on lunchmeat sandwiches and potato chips.

After lunch, Larry suggested they take the truck and see how far they could get with it. Even Dasher was invited on the foray. They were like little kids being offered ice cream and a movie, but their optimism was short-lived. A large tree had fallen near the check-in building and blocked the campground entrance. As Larry backed the truck to the intersection with the campground loop where he could turn around, he said, "I forgot the gate is locked anyway."

Mickey tried to lift their spirits. "We could have busted through. Well, we don't want to escape too soon because I have a great Christmas Eve meal planned. But I need firewood. We didn't think we'd have a fire until after we leave Bob and Lois's, so we didn't bring any. I bet we can find enough fallen stuff in the woods."

"If we go on a firewood expedition, we could cut an evergreen branch for a small Christmas tree," Frannie suggested from the back seat.

"Actually, pine branches would be good for the fire, too," Mickey said.

"The trick will be keeping a fire going in this wind," Larry said.

CHAPTER SEVEN
O Tannenbaum

THEY HEADED TOWARD the woods pulling a large plastic tote with a rope. The sun was out intermittently and the wind less insistent, producing a winter wonderland. Frannie regretted not grabbing her sunglasses. Dasher pranced along beside them, exuberant to be out and stretching her legs.

Numerous tracks punctured the otherwise pristine snow cover. She recognized deer and raccoon prints. There were others she wasn't anxious to identify. They laughed and joked but also kept a wary eye out for the owner of the blanket.

The wind still stung their faces, and they pulled scarves up over their mouths.

Branches that fell in the storm lay on top or close to the surface of the snow. Many were far too large for their purposes but they managed to collect enough shorter pieces to fill their tote. Dasher grabbed at a couple with her mouth, thinking they were working up to a game of fetch. Mickey found a couple of beautiful pines with branches sweeping the ground.

"How are we going to cut them?" Frannie said. "I don't think we can just break them off."

Mickey grinned and produced a pair of pruners from his jacket pocket. "Always prepared! I keep a pair in the coach to trim firewood if I need to. That's how I'm able to build those wonderful fires."

Larry scoffed. One of their longest standing arguments was over whether to build a teepee- or log-cabin-style fire.

Jane Ann and Frannie chose a branch that would make a good tabletop Christmas tree. Then they searched for small pinecones to use as decorations ,and Mickey cut some branches to add to his fire.

As they started back toward the campground, Mickey burst into "O Tannenbaum." His rich deep voice was such a contrast to his usual snarky self, that it never failed to amaze all of them, even his wife.

Frannie spotted a group of gray dogwood bushes and borrowed Mickey's pruners to cut a few branches with the whitish-gray berries. As she did, she noticed a bundle in the snow behind the bushes and up against a tree.

"Larry."

He backtracked a few steps to join her.

"Is that the blanket you saw?"

"Looks like it." He pushed through the bushes and picked up a corner.

"Omigod!" Frannie said.

"What?" Jane Ann and Mickey stopped and turned back.

"There's someone in that blanket."

"Jane Ann, come here," Larry said. "Check this guy."

Larry uncovered a face, which could be old or young, bluish skin bristling with an unkempt black beard. Jane Ann had spent years as a surgical nurse before retirement, and she bent to find a pulse. She looked up at Larry. "It's very faint but we need to get him inside as soon as possible. How can we move him?"

"We need a stretcher," Larry said. "C'mon Frannie — we'll see what we can cobble together. Jane Ann, is there anything else we can bring back?"

"Blankets," she said.

They both took hold of the rope to tow the box and trudged back toward their campsites.

"We could have left it until later," Frannie said as she struggled for breath in the cold air.

"We could have but we might need the rope or the box or both." He glanced at her. "You doing okay?"

"Yeah — just my usual problem. Out of shape. What's your guess about this guy?"

"Well, I don't think he's a threat. Probably a homeless guy who's been using the shower house as a warm place to sleep. Until we arrived."

They trudged through the snow in silence to conserve their breath. When they reached the campsites, Larry dumped the wood out on the ground and looked around.

"You want to get the blankets?"

"Sure. You know, there's that old flagpole in the front compartment that we could use for one side of a stretcher."

"Great idea." He continued scanning their campsite for another pole or substitute.

When she came back out, he was working at opening the awning.

"What are you doing?"

"Getting the other side of the stretcher. Help me get this open."

She stacked the blankets in the empty wood tub and helped raise the other side of the awning.

"Now what?"

"We're going to unclip each strut at the bottom and rest them on the ground. Then I'll just pull the bottom sliding part out of this one."

"Brilliant."

He looked at her with suspicion.

"I mean it."

They worked as quickly as they could and soon were headed back with the flagpole, an awning strut, and a pile of blankets. While they walked, Larry pulled his phone out and punched a few buttons. He finally gave an exasperated sigh and tried another number. A message appeared on the screen.

"'No service,'" he read and shoved it back in his pocket. "Wouldn't you know? If someone was trying to *sell* me more service, they'd get through."

Jane Ann was trying to warm the man's hands with her own and Mickey had taken his parka off and laid it over the silent form.

"You're going to end up in the same shape, Mick. Then who will cook us supper?" Frannie threw him one of the blankets. She and Larry took another one and tied it to the pole and strut.

"Hey," Mickey said. "That looks like one of your awning thingies."

"Exactly." Larry carried the makeshift stretcher over by Jane Ann.

She moved out of the way. "Be as gentle as you can when you move him. Did you try to call for help?"

Larry nodded. "No service. We'll try again when we get back. Mickey, can you get his feet? Put your coat back on and we'll cover him with the extra blankets."

Mickey did, and then he and Larry lifted the man onto the stretcher. Each of the four took one end of a pole or strut and lifted on the count of three.

They were only about a two-block walk from their campsites, but by the time they were halfway there, Frannie felt like her arms were going to pull out of their sockets and her fingers fall off. She gritted her teeth and told herself to be glad she wasn't the man who needed a stretcher. No one spoke; it took all of their concentration and effort to keep the stretcher as level as possible and still slog forward.

Finally they reached Ferraros' coach. They managed to get the stretcher inside and the man off-loaded onto the couch.

Jane Ann took charge. "Mickey, put a pan of water on the stove. We need to get some humidity in the air. And I need a pair of your sweatpants and a stocking cap. His jeans are wet from the snow."

"What can I do?" Frannie asked.

"You guys have an electric blanket, right? Why don't you go get it? We can run it off the generator." She took the stocking cap from Mickey and pulled it over the man's head. "Larry and Mickey, I'll need you guys to help me get his jeans off and those sweat pants on."

Frannie ran to get the electric blanket from her camper and put Dasher inside. When she returned, Jane Ann removed some of the blankets and tucked the electric blanket around him. "Mickey, have we got any kind of liquid we can heat up for him if he comes to? Nothing caffeine."

Mickey opened one of the cabinets and searched the labels. He held up a can. "Beef broth?"

"Perfect," Jane Ann said. He poured it into a saucepan with a little water to heat on the stove.

Larry tried his phone again with no luck. "I'll go out and try and get a fire going. You sure you want to do this big supper, Mickey?"

"Hey, we gotta eat, and what I have in mind won't take long. Maybe by then our guest will be able to take a little nourishment."

Jane Ann shook her head. "He needs hospital care—there's only so much we can do without power or medical equipment. He should have warm fluids by IV…"

Frannie rubbed her own hands together, still trying to get warmth back into them. "What else can I do?"

Jane Ann looked up. "Nothing right now."

"Do you need more blankets?"

"Not really."

Mickey had gone out to help Larry with the fire, and the arguments were already starting.

"I'll see if they need anything, then I'll be back."

"Good luck."

OUTSIDE, LARRY AND MICKEY were dragging the picnic table over to the fire.

"I don't think you'll get any of us to eat outside," Frannie said.

"Watch and learn, woman," Mickey said.

When they got it near the fire, they each took an end of the bench on the far side and, with grunts and dramatics, tipped it up.

Frannie smiled. "Ahhh—a windbreak."

Mickey strutted around to the fire and fanned it, bringing small bursts of flame. Then he pulled a very large cast-iron skillet out of a storage compartment.

"So what is on the menu?" Frannie asked. "If you'd stop being so stubborn and tell me, I could help."

He set the skillet on the ground, stood up and took a deep breath. "Paella."

"Wow," Frannie said. "So you want the chicken and what else from our fridge?"

"I think we'll save the meatballs and use chicken, chorizo and shrimp. You have peas, too? Any rice?"

"Yeah—a packaged mixed rice in the pantry. I'll see if Jane Ann needs anything and then I'll help cook."

Mickey gazed off in the distance. "What would really be great for this dish is some rabbit."

Frannie followed his stare. A fat gray rabbit sat watching them about twenty feet from the campsite.

"Mickey! You wouldn't! After all of the care you took of that poor bird, you can't kill a rabbit on Christmas Eve Day! Little friends of the forest and all that."

"I guess not." He sighed. "That reminds me, I'd better check our bird friend when I get things going here."

Larry was staring at his phone. "I have three bars right now!" He punched in the ranger's number and waited. They all held their breath until finally Larry said "Yes! This is Larry Shoemaker out at the campground, and we have an emergency."

CHAPTER EIGHT
We Need a Little Christmas

WHEN LARRY PUT his phone away, his face looked more relaxed than Frannie had seen him since the ice storm started the day before. "She said they should have the road open by evening. If not, they'll try and get a medevac chopper in here. And the power's supposed to be back on pretty soon."

Mickey and Frannie cheered, and Frannie went back in to tell Jane Ann.

"What's all the ruckus?"

"Larry got through to the ranger. They hope to have things open this evening."

"Great! If you'll stay here with our friend, I'm going to run over to the restroom." Frannie took a seat on a footstool near the couch.

When Jane Ann returned, they talked in low tones about being rescued.

"It hasn't really been too bad." Jane Ann pulled the scrunchie out of her ponytail, smoothed her still-blonde hair, and tied it back again.

"Now that we know we won't be stranded here forever."

"Yes, that helps." She shuffled through a stack of CDs and put on a disc of guitar holiday music. The strains of "I Wonder as I Wander" floated through the camper. "We've certainly done a lot of wandering and wondering in the last twenty-four hours."

"I think it's going to be a good Christmas, though. I just feel it—" Frannie straightened and stared at the man's face. "His eyelids just fluttered!"

The man coughed and raised his head. His eyes shut again and his head dropped back on the pillow.

"That's a good sign," Jane Ann said. "Go ahead if you want to do something else. I'll sit with him."

Frannie gave up the stool. "Mickey said I could help with supper."

Jane Ann raised her eyebrows. "That's a compliment. Usually he won't let anyone help him.

Is he going to tell you what you're cooking or make you do it blindfolded?"

"He announced it when I was out there. Paella."

"Oh yum. We'll eat in here. I'll clear the table and set things up while I keep an eye on him."

Frannie went back outside where Mickey fussed with the fire.

"More good news. The guy woke up a little bit—opened his eyes."

"Jane Ann can cure anyone," Mickey said with pride. Then, in case they thought he was getting soft, he added, "He's probably scared of what she'll do to him if he doesn't get better."

"Yeah, yeah," Frannie said. "Okay, give me a job."

"This is an important one." Mickey leaned his fire poker against the upturned table. "I want you to rub that chicken with a little paprika, oregano, pepper and salt and let it sit in the fridge for about an hour."

"How much of each of those?" Frannie liked her recipes to be precise.

"A little."

"Thanks."

Mickey picked up a couple of pine boughs to put on the fire.

"Not that one! That's our Christmas tree." She took the designated branch away from him.

"How can you tell?"

"I just can." She laid it on the ground by her camper and went inside. Dasher was more than excited to see her and spun in circles in the small space. The dog was especially interested in the chicken that she pulled from the fridge.

"Forget it," she said, and proceeded to follow Mickey's instructions. Then she searched in the pantry cupboard and found a bag of round pretzels. She put it in a bag along with some red yarn from her knitting, several plastic grocery bags, a red bandana, and an empty cottage cheese tub.

By this time, Dasher had forgotten about the unpleasant temperatures outside and waited by the door as Frannie put her coat on.

"Okay," she said to the dog, "but you have to stay outside with the men. It won't be pleasant, but that's how it is."

Outside, she picked up the little pine bough and took her treasures over to Jane Ann's. She was surprised to find her sister-in-law spoon-feeding the broth to the man, who was partially sitting up. He still wore the stocking cap but had improved enough that she could see that he was fairly young--in his twenties or early thirties. He looked pretty drowsy, but Jane Ann chatted away trying to keep him awake.

"Hi!" she said to Frannie. "Our friend says to call him JC. I told him that we hope an ambulance will be here soon, but he is doing better, thank goodness! This is my friend and sister-in-law, Frannie," she said to JC. She noticed Frannie's armload. "What do you have there?"

"Our Christmas tree." Frannie laid the branch and bag on the counter. She propped the branch in the plastic tub with the grocery bags stuffed around it. Then she arranged the bandana around the tub to camouflage it.

"Have you got ornaments, too?" Jane Ann asked, just as her patient started to cough. She laid the spoon and mug aside. "Here—let's sit up a little more." She supported his back. "Frannie, bring me a couple of paper towels."

Jane Ann used them to wipe his mouth, and then he lay back on the pillow, waving the broth away.

"I saw the star." His voice was high and raspy and very faint, and he was looking at Frannie.

Jane Ann looked at Frannie and shrugged. "What?" Frannie asked him.

"The star in the window," he said.

"Ohhh," Frannie said, " —the lighted star in the window of the camper?" He had to be talking about the night before when they still had power. "You were outside?"

"Not long."

Frannie remembered one of the stories of her childhood, *The Little Matchgirl,* a gruesome Hans Christian Anderson tale about a little girl who freezes to death while watching a wealthy family at Christmas through their lighted windows. She shuddered.

"You should rest," she said, because she didn't know what else to say.

"Frannie's right," Jane Ann said. "Do you want any more broth?" He shook his head. "Don't go to sleep, but try and rest. Don't exert yourself."

Frannie busied herself tying pretzels, pinecones, and berries to the little tree with the red yarn. When she finished, she set the little tree in the middle of the dinette table.

"The perfect touch!" Jane Ann said. She got up and put a Mannheim Steamroller CD on the player.

"The Carol of the Bells" was just pealing out when Mickey came in. "The bird has flown the coop." He beamed, and then sobered a little. "I'm going to assume that some other animal didn't get it."

"Mickey, this is JC," Jane Ann said.

"JC?" He sounded incredulous.

"Yes. Why?"

"It's Christmas."

It dawned on Frannie first. "Oh." She looked at Jane Ann. "Did he give you his full name?"

"Jacob Carrera," Jane Ann said and smiled at their guest who seemed puzzled at this exchange. "My husband thought you were Jesus Christ."

JC gave a weak smile. "Hardly."

"Okay. Well." Mickey dusted off his hands. "I won't have to watch myself then. Time to get some prep done for our feast." He got out a cutting board and started to chop an onion. "Frannie, you can go ahead and cut that chicken into strips."

"Okay. Will you have room on the fire for another pot?"

"No problem. What are you making?"

"It's a Christmas secret."

Mickey grumped, but Jane Ann said, "Serves you right, Mick."

"I have a bag of spinach too, and some Clementines. I'll make a salad," Frannie said.

OUTSIDE, LARRY WAS tending the fire. Frannie put her arm around his waist.

"I think you need an inside job for a while. We don't need two hypothermia cases."

Larry looked around. The dusk was deepening, silhouetting the bare trees against the pink and gold sunset. "If not for the cold and wind, it's a beautiful evening." He smiled. "You're right—I am ready for an inside job. What have you got for me?"

"You can mix up some spiced cider while I cut up the chicken."

He put his arm around her shoulders as they walked toward the trailer. "So this is probably not what you had in mind for Christmas."

"You know what? It's been great! And it will get better." And as she said it, Mickey's rope lights along their path lit up and the outside light on their camper came on. So did the lights in the shower house.

"Wow! You must be a Christmas magician."

"Of course I am. How did you think I got all of the food ready, presents wrapped, and the house cleaned in the past?" She grinned, and the lights flicked off. "Oh, oh. I'd better shut up."

CHAPTER NINE
I Saw Three Ships

LARRY MIXED CIDER with maple syrup and spices in the cast-iron Dutch oven while Frannie peeled a few Clementines, threw a couple of the peels in the pot of cider, and mixed up salad dressing. Suddenly, the star in the kitchen window lit up again and the little space heater started to grind out some heat. Larry looked at Frannie. She said "Not a word!" and covered her mouth with her hand.

The star stayed lit and the heater continued to churn. "Yes!" Frannie whispered. Larry took the cider out to put on the fire, and Frannie cut up the chicken. When she took out the bowl, Mickey was heating oil in the skillet.

"About time! If you want to be my assistant, you need to show a little more responsibility, young lady."

"Oh, hush." She handed him the bowl of chicken. The pot of cider was perched on the little built-in grill at the side of the fire ring, so that Mickey could use his swing-away grill for the large skillet.

"I'm surprised you could get that post pounded into the ground," Larry said, indicating the grill support.

"Apparently, it hasn't been cold long enough here to have much frost in the ground."

"I'll go see how Jane Ann's doing with her patient. What else do you need?" Frannie said to Mickey.

"When you come back out, bring that tray that's on the counter. I'll be ready for the shrimp in about five minutes."

"Gotcha, Boss."

Jane Ann had reheated the rest of the broth and was helping JC take sips from the mug.

"So where are you from?" she asked.

"Um, Kansas City mostly."

"Do you have family around here?"

"No." His clipped answer said he didn't want to discuss it further.

MICKEY SCOOPED THE chicken out of the skillet and added the shrimp. While it was cooking, Frannie ladled out some mugs of cider to which Larry added a splash of rum. Larry went in to keep Jane Ann company and take her a mug. Frannie sipped hers, letting it warm her insides, and watched the stars come out in the endless black sky.

When the shrimp was done, Mickey removed it to another bowl and began browning the chorizo with garlic and onion and the rice mix. Frannie stood close enough to the fire to feel its warmth and savor the smells. Mickey snapped his fingers and pointed at the can of tomatoes, the water, and the bowl of chicken.

"Pretty bossy," she said, as she handed them to him.

He whistled "Jingle Bells" as he added the seasonings, stirred the whole mess, and put the lid on. He looked at his watch. "Ten minutes. Or so. Let's go inside. Is your salad ready?"

"I just need to throw it together. I'll get it." She went back to her own trailer. After combining the spinach, Clementines, and dressing in a bowl, she also arranged a plate of sugar cookies and peanut clusters. The sight of the chocolate lifted her spirits even more.

She carried the bowl and plate over to Mickey and Jane Ann's trailer. The men were back by the fire. Larry held a large bowl while Mickey spooned the colorful mixture into it. Dasher sat underneath the bowl, looking up hopefully.

"Look at that Christmas spirit. You're working together," Frannie said.

"Yeah, but Larry won't hold the bowl still," Mickey said.

"It's burning my hands," Larry complained.

"That's better," Frannie said. "That's the guys I love."

"See? She still thinks we're cute."

Larry grinned. "Told you it would work."

Frannie waved them off in disgust and went up the steps of the camper. Inside, Jane Ann had arranged chairs so that JC on the couch was included in the group. A small candle gave off a piney scent and more Christmas tunes came out of the CD player.

JC still lay with his head back and eyes half closed. "I wish that ambulance would get here," Jane Ann said. "I think he's going to be fine, but I would feel a lot better about it if he was under real medical care."

"Can he eat anything?" Frannie asked.

"Not solids. Mickey's going to pour some of the broth off the paella for him."

JC raised his eyes and looked at them. "I'll be okay. Thank you for helping me."

Jane Ann smiled at him. "Hey, don't give us too much credit. We're kind of a captive audience here."

He made a sound like a chuckle.

Larry and Mickey clambered in with the food, followed by Dasher.

"Oh, Larry, there isn't room for her too. Can you take her back to our place?" Frannie said.

"C'mon, Fran—it's Christmas. She'll be fine when we all sit down," Mickey said.

JC's face lit up. "Hey, pooch." Dasher whined and wiggled under the table to get to JC and lick his face.

"Have you seen her before? Is she yours?" Jane Ann asked.

"We been hanging out—she's a bum like me. But she disappeared last night." JC looked exhausted from the effort of his answer.

"She came to our door. You should have too," Frannie said.

Mickey opened a bottle of Merlot and poured four glasses. "What about him?" he said quietly to Jane Ann.

"No alcohol," she said. She turned to CD player down low and they jockeyed around to take their places at the table. Mickey filled their plates while Jane Ann helped JC with a few sips of the fragrant broth.

"Good," he said.

"This is really amazing, especially for a snowbound meal," Frannie said. They raised their glasses in a toast. Mickey said a short grace and they all dug in.

"Mickey, I know this will go to your head, but this is fantastic," Frannie said. "Best Christmas Eve meal I've ever had."

"Hey, I smoked a brisket for you last Christmas ,and we did lobster the year before."

"Yeah, but this is special."

"It really is good, Mick," Larry said.

Jane Ann put down her fork in shock. "Wow, it *must* be Christmas." She noticed JC's puzzled look. "They never say anything nice to each other. Do you have brothers or sisters?"

"One sister. I get it."

"I wish we could share some of this with you."

He shook his head. "Not that hungry. The broth is good."

"I was just thinking, Jane Ann, about that year that Bob wouldn't get up Christmas morning so that we could open our presents. Remember that?" Larry said.

Jane Ann laughed. "Dad went in and poured water on his head. I don't know who was the maddest—Bob or Mom because he soaked the bedding."

"Your dad was quite a practical joker in those days, wasn't he?" Frannie asked.

"He was terrible. Family, neighbors, friends—nobody was safe from his pranks."

JC laughed. Not a full belly laugh, but a laugh nonetheless. "My dad, too. Salt in the sugar bowl, stuff like that."

"One time—," Jane Ann began, but stopped to listen. She reached up and turned off the music. A distant rumble punctuated by a siren reached their ears. Jane Ann had closed the shades to help insulate the camper from the cold so Larry raised the one on the big dinette window.

Flashes of red and blue reflected off the trees and as they watched, a white strobe came around the corner atop a huge snowplow, followed by a highway patrol car and an ambulance. They all tried to get up at once, resulting in a spilled glass of wine and dropped silverware, but nobody cared.

Mickey was the first out the door and the rest tumbled after, grabbing coats as they went. Dasher raced toward the plow, barking frantically. The snowplow stopped just past their campsites so the ambulance could pull in. Ranger Hart jumped out of the patrol car and rushed over to them.

"I'm so sorry," she said. "I didn't know it was going to get this bad. Ooof!" She jumped as Dasher barreled into the back of her knees. She turned and saw who her attacker was. "Well, hey, girl. Have you been hanging out here too?"

"Do you know this dog?" Larry asked. "She showed up on our doorstep last night, and we couldn't leave her out in the storm."

"She's around here a lot, especially in the summer, but she belongs to a farm down the road. We'll drop her off when we leave."

Jane Ann directed the EMTs into the camper while Mickey added to the fire and they huddled around, trying to stay out of the way. Frannie's phone rang. It was their son Sam.

"Hello, Mom? Is that a siren?" As if on cue, the driver shut the klaxon down.

"Um, yeah, but we're fine. Merry Christmas!"

"What's going on? I tried calling the house phone but nobody answered. The kids wanted to talk to you."

"We're on our way to Uncle Bob's with Mickey and Jane Ann."

"Tonight?" Sam said. "Why didn't you go earlier?"

"Good question. Listen, can we call you back in about half an hour? We're really all fine but kind of busy right this minute."

Sam was hesitant. "Sure. But you are all okay?"

"Absolutely. Love you all and talk to you soon."

He hung up. "Sam," she said to Larry's questioning look.

The EMTs were bringing JC out and strapping him to a gurney. They covered him with a heavy blanket and half-rolled, half-carried the gurney to the ambulance. JC whispered, "Thanks" as he rolled past the group. One of the EMTs took down information from Jane Ann.

"Where will you be taking him?"

"The regional hospital in Rock City."

"We'll stop by tomorrow and check on him before we head out," she said.

"Good. I would say you saved his life."

"That's why we carry a nurse when we camp," Mickey said.

The EMT looked a little puzzled, but shrugged and thanked them and joined the crew in the ambulance. As it pulled away, Frannie noticed that the two guys from the snowplow had joined them.

"Thank you so much!" Frannie told them. "We were doing okay but it could have turned really bad at any time. Would you like some hot cider?" She indicated the pot at the side of the fire.

"No," said one, a big guy with red curly hair and a redder face. "We need to get back to town and get some supper. Been out on the roads since 4:00 this morning."

"Then let me get you a plate. We have some fantastic paella that my brother-in-law whipped up and he makes enough for an army — or a road crew."

"Welll —" Red looked at his companion, a small wiry man with stringy brown hair protruding from his stocking cap. "What d'you think, Kyle?"

"Sounds great if it isn't too much trouble."

"No trouble at all. Do you want to come inside?"

"Actually, it's pretty nice here by the fire," Red said.

Frannie laughed. "I guess you're dressed for it." She eyed their bulky coveralls. "Be right back."

She filled two plates and reheated them in the microwave. While she waited, she mopped up the spilled wine. Fortunately it had been contained on the table. She carried the plates and forks back outside. Jane Ann had gotten Kelly Hart and the patrolman mugs of cider — sans rum. Dasher lived up to her name racing around the campsite.

"What about you? Could you use a little supper?" Frannie asked Kelly and the patrolman.

"I just ate," said Kelly, "but that looks heavenly. Could I just try a little bit?"

"I'll have a whole plate," said the patrolman. "No supper for me tonight."

"Coming right up."

Soon they were all standing around the fire, loading forkfuls of paella into their mouths and exclaiming over the dish.

"Oh, pshaw," Mickey said, feigning embarrassment. "It was nothing."

"Humility doesn't become you, Ferraro," Larry said.

The patrolman asked more about how they had found JC and what they knew about him.

"Really, not much," Jane Ann said. "He's from Kansas City and has one sister."

"Well, good thing you found him. I don't think he'd have made it through another night."

Larry set his empty plate on the camper steps. "Apparently he's been sleeping in the shower house. So if we hadn't stopped here, he probably would have been fine. The least we could do was rescue him."

Frannie collected the empty plates and took them inside. When she returned, she handed around the plate of cookies and peanut clusters. More accolades followed until their guests said they needed to get back on the job. Ranger Hart promised to be back early in the morning. They all said their goodbyes to everyone, especially Dasher.

"We'd better call Sam," Larry said after they left. "I'm sure he's wondering what's going on."

"Serves him right," Frannie said with a grin. "Think of all the nights we sat up and wondered the same thing when he was a teenager." But she pulled out her phone and made the call. She gave him a condensed version of their adventure and fended off most of his questions with another assurance that they were fine.

"Now let me talk to my grandchildren."

Sarabeth (nicknamed Sabet by her little brother) got on first and chronicled their day at Disney World in great detail. Frannie could hear Joe in the background saying "I wanna tell *that*!" so she finally cut Sabet off with "You can tell me more about it when you get back. I'd better talk to Joe and then you can both wish Grandpa a Merry Christmas." By this time she was stomping her feet to warm them and walking in circles.

She handed the phone to Larry after a short visit with Joe. Jane Ann had called Bob and updated him on their plans for departure the next day.

"I'll help with the dishes," Frannie said.

"That would be great," Jane Ann said. "I thought about leaving them until morning but that's probably not such a good idea."

They went inside, and while the water was heating on the stove, they folded up the blankets JC had been using and sorted them out. Frannie made a stack to take back to her own camper. While they did the dishes, they chatted about their upcoming visit with Bob and Lois, and, later, one of Mickey and Jane Ann's daughters, Justine, in west Texas.

"This is her first Christmas that she hasn't come home, but she's had too much trouble with this pregnancy to travel, so it will be great to see her."

Larry stuck his head in the door. "Are you chicks coming back out, or should we let the fire go out?"

"We'll be back out in a second. Why don't you take that stack of blankets back to our trailer?"

Larry grabbed the stack and muttered "Work, work, work" as he closed the door.

Outside, Frannie ladled herself one more mug of cider while Mickey tuned up his guitar. He had thrown about a foot of old Christmas lights in the fire, creating flames of blue, green and purple.

"What are we singing?" she asked.

"Just one." And he started into "Silent Night." They all sang and the harmony seemed pretty good — since there wasn't an audience.

When they finished, Mickey put the guitar away. Frannie impulsively hugged him, Jane Ann, and finally her husband. "Merry Christmas," she whispered, because she didn't want to disturb the silence.

The rest responded in kind and gazed at the crisp, starry night. Frannie thought this was the most beautiful Christmas she had ever seen.

CHAPTER TEN
Let it Begin with Me

THE NEXT MORNING, Frannie woke curled into Larry's back with an immense feeling of contentment. The sun was starting to filter through the blinds; she had slept much longer than usual. They would have a long day of driving ahead of them. They had checked the weather the night before, and there were no storms headed toward them. JC was safely in the hospital, and Dasher was back with her family. Life was good.

She finally decided to give up her warm cocoon and stuck her feet out of the covers. Not too bad, so she got up and took her clothes out to the living room to dress. More room out there. She plugged the old electric percolator in—no gritty coffee this morning—and put her coat and boots on to head to the shower house. The remaining snow on the trees had crystalized and produced a fairyland under the intense blue sky.

Sometimes she needed to lose or almost lose something to really appreciate it. The warm shower house, hot running water, and, when she returned, a pot of hot, strong coffee were wonderful Christmas gifts. She retrieved a loaf of cranberry bread from the fridge and warmed it in the microwave. Instant oatmeal in a paper bowl would save on dishes, and she was almost done eating when Larry appeared, scratching his back and yawning.

"Merry Christmas," he said.

"I think it is," she said, "and the same to you."

He leaned over and kissed her. "Heard anything from the Ferraros this morning?"

"Not yet. I'll text Jane Ann when I finish my breakfast."

He looked at the clock. "I'd like to be on the road by 9:00. We want to stop at the hospital, right? So after I get something to eat, I'll get ready to hook up."

"Okay by me. I'll start putting stuff away in here."

While she was doing that, her phone rang and it was their daughter Sally. It was almost the end of her Christmas Day in Switzerland, and she was full of happiness and good wishes. Frannie gave her an abbreviated version of their attempt to get to Texas and promised her full details when she brought Brett to the house later in January. She handed the phone to Larry, filled with a warm feeling, and wondered why she had been so put out with Sally earlier.

She filled her travel mug, topped off Larry's, and cleaned up the coffee pot. Mickey and Jane Ann burst in with Christmas greetings and hugs. Frannie passed around warm, buttered slices of bread while they discussed their route to Oklahoma, their target for the day.

Once they had completed the arduous task of hooking up the truck in the bitter cold, they stomped their feet, rubbed their hands, and climbed into their vehicles. When they reached the campground entrance, the large tree had been removed and cut. Chunks lay alongside the road. Lights were on in the registration shack and Kelly Hart waved to them as they passed out of the park.

THE SMALL, ONE-FLOOR hospital sat on the edge of town back from the road. A large parking lot to one side provided plenty of space for their RVs. The lobby exploded with a bedlam of holiday decorations, many looking like castoffs from the employees' homes. A few people were standing or seated in groups; some sharing holiday joy and others sadness. Mickey went up to the information desk and asked for Jacob Carrera's room.

They were directed down a long hall to another reception area and eventually to a doorway festooned with silver rope tinsel and an elf dressed in felt whose smirking face seemed to be taunting anyone who entered. The door stood partially open, and Jane Ann pushed it further.

"JC?"

He looked up from the bed nearest the door, and his face brightened when he saw her.

"Hi."

They were all the way in the room before Frannie noticed a young woman sitting in the only chair back against the wall.

"Kath, these are the people who rescued me."

She smiled, got up, and held out her hand. "Thank you so much for what you did. I'm JC's sister."

"She should be home with her own family. It is Christmas, after all," JC said.

"My kids told me not to come home without Uncle JC. They are releasing him some time this morning."

"Wonderful!" Jane Ann said. "Do you live in Kansas City too?"

Kath shook her head. "St. Louis. So, I understand you were on your way somewhere for the holidays and got stranded by the storm?"

"We sure did. We were supposed to be at our brother's in Texas by yesterday. So we'll be on our way this morning, but wanted to see how JC was doing," Larry said.

"Well, you've made this a very merry Christmas for me. I have two kids and they are going to be so excited to see him. The doctor said only mild to moderate hypothermia, and that he was very lucky not to have been out there any longer."

JC looked uncomfortable. "Kath, don't talk their leg off. They probably want to get going."

"It's not that big of a rush," Mickey said. "We're retired and not on any schedule."

A doctor appeared in the doorway, brandishing a clipboard. "Wow!" he said. "I didn't know it was a party. I didn't dress for it."

Kath said, "Doctor, these are the people who found JC yesterday."

He shook their hands. "You did an excellent job. I'm just here to check him out and hopefully release him to go have a real Christmas."

"We'll get out of your way. We just wanted to say good-bye," Frannie said.

"Go right ahead." The doctor made a sweeping gesture.

One by one, they went to the bed and said their farewells. Jane Ann and Frannie each gave him a kiss on the forehead, Larry shook his hand, and Mickey patted him on the shoulder.

"I'll walk out with you so the doctor can check him out," Kath said.

WHEN THEY WERE well away from the door, Kath said, "My brother has been missing for four months. He came back from Afghanistan with PTSD and resisted any therapy or treatment. Couldn't hold a job and took off in August. I filed a missing persons report but didn't get any word until last night."

"Did the police call you?" Frannie asked.

"No, JC gave the hospital my number and asked them to." She started to cry but smiled through her tears. "He told me this morning that being around you people made him realize how important family is."

"I think that's the first time anyone has considered us exemplary," Jane Ann said drily. "Anyone listening to my husband and brother would think they hated each other."

Kath shook her head. "Not really. JC saw through that. It was great what you did for him."

It was Larry's turn to shake his head. "If he's a vet, what we did doesn't compare to his sacrifice. Please, thank him from us for his service."

"I hope he can get the help he needs," Jane Ann said.

"He agreed this morning to at least try. Thank you again and have a great holiday." She pressed a card into Jane Ann's hand. "My email address is on there. Please let me know when you arrive safely. JC will wonder." She gave them each a hug and hurried back down the hallway to her brother's room.

WHEN THEY REACHED the main lobby, the receptionist hailed them over. "Are you the—" she looked at a slip of paper on her desk—"Shoemakers and the Ferraros?"

"Yes," Frannie said. "Is something wrong?"

"I don't think so, but a patrolman and a park ranger were asking about you."

"Where did they go?" Larry asked.

"Well, I'm not sure because I got busy. They might have gone back outside."

"Did they leave a message?"

"No, they didn't."

"Okay, thanks."

They walked outside and headed for their vehicles at the far side of the lot.

"There's something on our truck—on the front," Frannie said.

As they got closer, Jane Ann laughed. "It's a Christmas wreath attached to the grill. Look, there's one on our coach, too."

When they reached the truck, Larry noticed a yellow slip of paper stuck under the windshield wiper. "What! A ticket! That's a nice gift. I didn't see any signs about parking here." He scanned the lot again.

Frannie reached up and dislodged the paper. It was a traffic ticket form but was blank. On the back was written "Merry Christmas and safe travels!"

LATER, AS THEY rolled down the interstate, Frannie said, "Life is funny."

Larry smiled at her. "That's profound."

"I just mean how things turn out. I was so bummed about Sam and Sally not coming home for Christmas, and then we hit an ice storm and get snowbound and lose power and I think it is one of the best Christmases ever."

"Yeah, it's funny how that works." He reached over and patted her hand and then turned up the radio. John Lennon's voice singing "Happy Christmas (War is Over)" filled the cab.

Happy Holiday Camper Tip #1

MICKEY'S CASSEROLE BREAD

A quick bread that is also healthy!

1 1/2 cups whole wheat flour
1 cup all-purpose flour
1/2 cup quick-cooking rolled oats
1/3 cup brown sugar, packed
1 tablespoon finely grated orange peel
2 teaspoon baking powder
1/2 teaspoon baking soda
1 3/4 cups buttermilk
1 egg white
2 tablespoon sunflower nuts
wheat germ
honey

Combine flours, oats, sugar, orange peel, baking powder, and baking soda until well-blended. Add buttermilk and egg white and stir until just moistened. Stir in the sunflower nuts.

Spray a 1 1/2 quart casserole and sprinkle with wheat germ. Pour batter into casserole and bake 50-60 minutes at 350°. Cool for 15 minutes and turn out on wire rack. Brush top with honey and sprinkle with more sunflower nuts.

Happy Holiday Camper Tip #2

FRANNIE'S SUGAR COOKIES

I have disputed the characteristics of Real Sugar Cookies with several friends through the years. The ones I grew up with were rolled as thin as possible and decorated only with red or green sugar, never frosting or sprinkles or other unnecessaries. This is the recipe. I always double it.

2 cups all-purpose flour
1 cup sugar
1/4 teaspoon salt
1/2 teaspoon baking powder
1/2 cup softened butter
1 egg
2 tablespoons brandy, rum, or whiskey (or 1 tablespoon each milk and lemon juice)
1/2 teaspoon vanilla

Stir dry ingredients together. Add butter and mix with fingers until coarse crumbs. Add egg and liquor. Add vanilla and knead until dough holds together. Form into a ball, wrap in plastic wrap, and refrigerate until chilled enough to handle. Roll out on a floured surface to about 1/8" thick. Cut with cookie cutters, place on greased cookie sheets, sprinkle with sugar and bake 5-10 minutes in a 400° oven.

Happy Holiday Camper Tip #3

OH, THE WEATHER OUTSIDE IS FRIGHTFUL ...!

Insulation: Most trailers and RVs are not insulated the way a house is. If you travel in the winter you can benefit from a couple of simple tricks. Vent insulators, or vent cushions, are available from RV stores, simply push into the vent area, and prevent the loss of precious heat. They can also be used in the summer to keep direct sun out when using the AC.

Windows are always a prominent cause of heat loss. Bubble wrap—the larger the bubbles, the better—can be cut to fit the window glass, sprayed with water, and smoothed over the glass until no longer needed.

Happy Holiday Camper Tip #4

MULLED APPLE CIDER

In a crockpot or saucepan, heat apple cider. Add a little brown sugar or maple syrup, cloves, cinnamon sticks and allspice. If you use whole spices, tie them up in a little cheesecloth bag. Add an orange peel. Simmer. Serve with a little rum, if desired.

Happy Holiday Camper Tip #5

MICKEY'S PAELLA IN A PINCH

   2 tablespoons olive oil
   2 skinned and deboned chicken breasts, cut in strips
   1 pound medium shrimp, peeled and deveined
   1 pound chorizo
   1 medium onion, finely chopped
   2 cloves garlic, minced
   2 packages Minute multi-grain medley
   1 cup instant long grain, brown, and wild rice mix
   1/4 teaspoon paprika
   1/4 teaspoon turmeric
   1 can of diced tomatoes or pint of tomato sauce
   2 14.5 oz. cans reduced-sodium chicken broth
   Coarse salt and ground pepper
   1 cup frozen green peas, thawed
   1 lemon

1. Rub the chicken breast with a little sweet paprika, dried oregano, coarse salt and ground pepper. Refrigerate for about an hour. Cut into strips.

2. In a heavy cast iron skillet, heat 1 tablespoon oil over the fire. Cook the chicken strips for about 5 minutes and reserve. Cook shrimp until just pink on both sides, 4 to 5 minutes (do not overcook). Transfer to a plate.

3. Add remaining tablespoon oil and chorizo to pan; cook over medium-high heat until beginning to brown, about 2 minutes. Add onion and stir until translucent.

Add garlic and rice; cook, stirring to coat, until rice is translucent, 1 to 2 minutes.

4. Stir in paprika, turmeric, tomatoes, chicken and broth, scraping up browned bits from bottom of pan with a wooden spoon. Season with salt and pepper.

5. Bring to a boil, then reduce heat to a simmer. Cover, and cook until rice is tender and has absorbed almost all liquid, 10 minutes. Stir in peas; cook 1 minute. Stir in cooked shrimp; serve immediately.

Makes enough for four plus a road crew.

Happy Holiday Camper Tip #6

ENDING THE DRAFT

A temporary fix for drafts is painters tape. If you are going to be in a campsite for several days, and you have a bad cold air draft behind a cabinet, or appliance, place some painters tape over the spot, and get immediate relief. And the tape will come off later easily without leaving any glue.

Happy Holiday Camper Tip #7

CLEANING CAST IRON

Most cast iron cooks know that soap can affect the flavor of foods cooked in cast iron. One easy recommended method is to sprinkle the pan with salt and rub it around. Add a little olive oil and continue rubbing. Wash it with water and dry thoroughly.

Happy Holiday Camper Tip #8

SPINACH SALAD WITH CLEMENTINES

   6 cups baby spinach leaves
   12 clementines, sectioned
   1/2 cup walnut or pecan pieces
   1 bunch green onions, sliced crosswise (optional)
   1/2 cup sliced water chestnuts (optional)

   For the dressing:
   3 tablespoons olive oil
   juice of two limes or lemons (about 1/4 cup)
   1 tablespoon Dijon mustard

Mix salad ingredients together. Shake dressing ingredients in a small jar and pour over salad.

Happy Holiday Camper Tip #9

CHOCOLATE PEANUT CLUSTERS

Melt 1 12 oz package of chocolate chips and 2 1/4 pounds almond bark. Stir in 12 ounces salted Spanish peanuts. Drop by spoonfuls on wax paper to cool.

Happy Holiday Camper Tip #10

FRANNIE'S STONE SOUP

The great thing about soup is that you can make it out of almost anything. Good opportunity to clean out the fridge or have a group meal. Especially handy in a pinch are frozen meatballs, chicken strips, or summer sausage.

1 dozen frozen meatballs
1 or 2 cans of diced tomatoes
3 cans of water for every 1 can of diced tomatoes
frozen mixed veggies
Italian seasoning
beef broth or bullion
mushrooms, onions or whatever
stick to the ribs starchy stuff: whole wheat rotini, brown rice or barley

That's the basics. Dump it all in a crockpot or cast iron Dutch oven, except the rotini, rice or barley. Add that at the end and cook the required amount of time.

Bonus Happy Holiday Camper Tip

Finally, the Minnesota Department of Safety has excellent tips on their website for winter survival.

They include this list of items to keep in your vehicle. Use an empty three-pound coffee can or any similar container with a plastic cover to store the following items:

Small candles and matches
Small, sharp knife and plastic spoons
Red bandanna or cloth
Pencil and paper
Large plastic garbage bag
Safety pins
Whistle
Snacks
Cell phone adapter to plug into lighter
Plastic flashlight and spare batteries
https://dps.mn.gov/divisions/ots/educational-materials/Documents/Winter-Survival-Brochure.pdf

Acknowledgements

The experiences others have had while camping never cease to surprise me. When I began this novella, I queried people on several RV Facebook pages about winter camping and a number replied with harrowing tales about being snow bound, out of propane, and one about finding a person stranded by a storm. I thank everyone for your input.

My Beta readers for this one were Elaine, Ginge, Pam and my technical advisor, husband Butch. They made lots of great catches and asked lots of good questions. Their input was invaluable. And special thanks to Aurora Lightbourne for the great cover and Libby Shannon for formatting it.

The award-winning Frannie Shoemaker Campground Mysteries:

Bats and Bones: (An IndieBRAG Medallion honoree) Frannie and Larry Shoemaker are retirees who enjoy weekend camping with their friends in state parks. They anticipate the usual hiking, campfires, good food, and interesting side trips among the bluffs of beautiful Bat Cave State Park for the long Fourth of July weekend—until a dead body turns up. Confined in the campground and surrounded by strangers, Frannie is drawn into the investigation.

The Blue Coyote: (An IndieBRAG Medallion honoree and a 2013 Chanticleer CLUE finalist) Frannie and Larry Shoemaker love taking their grandchildren, Sabet and Joe, camping with them. But at Bluffs State Park, Frannie finds herself worrying more than usual about their safety, and when another young girl disappears from the campground in broad daylight, her fears increase. Accusations against Larry and her add to the cloud over their heads.

Peete and Repeat: (An IndieBRAG Medallion honoree, 2013 Chanticleer CLUE finalist, and 2014 Chanticleer Mystery and Mayhem finalist) A biking and camping trip to southeastern Minnesota turns into double trouble for Frannie Shoemaker and her friends as she deals with a canoeing mishap and a couple of bodies. Strange happenings in the campground, the nearby nature learning center, and an old power plant complicate the suspect pool and Frannie tries to stay out of it--really--but what can she do?

The Lady of the Lake: (An IndieBRAG Medallion honoree, 2014 Chanticleer CLUE finalist) A trip down memory lane is fine if you don't stumble on a body. Frannie Shoemaker and her friends camp at Old Dam Trail State Park near one of Donna Nowak's childhood homes and take in the county fair. But the present intrudes when a body surfaces. Donna becomes the focus of the investigation and Frannie wonders if the police shouldn't be looking closer at the victim's many enemies.

To Cache a Killer: Geocaching isn't supposed to be about finding dead bodies. But when retiree, Frannie Shoemaker go camping, standard definitions don't apply. A weekend in a beautiful state park in Iowa buzzes with fund-raising events, a search for Ninja turtles, a bevy of suspects, and lots of great food. But are the campers in the wrong place at the wrong time once too often?

The Space Invader: A cozy/thriller mystery! The starry skies over New Mexico, the "Land of Enchantment," may hold secrets of their own. The Shoemakers and the Ferraros, on an extended camping trip, find themselves picking up a souvenir they don't want and taking side trips they didn't plan on. Recipes and camping tips included.

THE TIME TRAVEL TRAILER SERIES

The Time Travel Trailer: (A Chanticleer 2015 Cygnus award finalist) A 1937 vintage camper trailer half hidden in weeds catches Lynne McBriar's eye when she is visiting an elderly friend Ben. Ben eagerly sells it to her and she just as eagerly embarks on a restoration. But after each remodel, sleeping in the trailer lands Lynne and her daughter Dinah in a previous decade — exciting, yet frightening. Glimpses of their home town and ancestors fifty or sixty years earlier is exciting and also offers some clues to the mystery of Ben's lost love. But when Dinah makes a trip on her own, she separates herself from her mother by decades. It is a trip that may upset the future if Lynne and her estranged husband can't team up to bring their daughter back.

Trailer on the Fly: How many of us have wished at some time or other we could go back in time and change an action or a decision or just take back something that was said? But it is what it is. There is no rewind, reboot, delete key or any other trick to change the past, right?

Lynne McBriar can. She bought a 1937 camper that turned out to be a time portal. And when she meets a young woman who suffers from serious depression over the loss of a close friend ten years earlier, she has the power to do something about it. And there is no reason not to use that power. Right?

ABOUT THE AUTHOR

Karen Musser Nortman is the author of the Frannie Shoemaker Campground cozy mystery series, including four BRAGMedallion honorees. After previous incarnations as a secondary social studies teacher (22 years) and a test developer (18 years), she returned to her childhood dream of writing a novel. The Frannie Shoemaker Campground Mysteries came out of numerous 'round the campfire' discussions, making up answers to questions raised by the peephole glimpses one gets into the lives of fellow campers. Where did those people disappear to for the last two days? What kinds of bones are in this fire pit? Why is that woman wearing heels to the shower house?

Karen and her husband Butch originally tent camped when their children were young and switched to a travel trailer when sleeping on the ground lost its romantic adventure. They take frequent weekend jaunts with friends to parks in Iowa and surrounding states, plus occasional longer trips. Entertainment on these trips has ranged from geocaching and hiking/biking to barbecue contests, balloon fests, and buck skinners' rendezvous.

Made in the USA
Middletown, DE
23 October 2023